# MEET THE GIRL TALK CHARACTERS

*Sabrina Wells* is petite, with curly auburn hair, sparkling hazel eyes, and a bubbly personality. Sabrina loves magazines, shopping, sleepovers, and most of all, she loves talking to her best friends.

*Katie Campbell* is a straight-A student and super athlete. With her blond hair, blue eyes, and matching clothes, she's everyone's idea of Little Miss Perfect. But Katie has a few surprises for everyone, including herself!

*Randy Zak* has just moved to Acorn Falls from New York City, and is she ever cool! With her radical spiked haircut and her hip New York clothes, Randy teaches everyone just how much fun it is to be different.

*Allison Cloud* is a Native American Indian. Allison's supersmart and really beautiful. But she has one major problem: She's thirteen years old, five foot seven, and still growing!

# ALLISON, SHAPE UP!

### By L. E. Blair

GIRL TALK® series created by Western Publishing Company, Inc.

Western Publishing Company, Inc., Racine, Wisconsin 53404

Text by B. B. Calhoun

# Chapter One

"Yuck," said Sabrina, plopping her tray down on the cafeteria table in front of her. "Meat loaf again. I wish they would serve pizza more often."

"That's why I like to bring my own lunch," said Katie, tucking a lock of her silky blond hair behind her ear and lifting a container of yogurt out of her lunch bag. "At least that way, I know what I'm getting."

"You're right," agreed Sabrina with a sigh. "But you have a cook to pack your lunch. Sometimes I just can't find the time to make my own lunch."

Sabrina Wells and Katie Campbell are two of my best friends. The three of us were sitting down to eat lunch together in the cafeteria at Bradley Junior High, where we're all in the seventh grade. Sabs and Katie and I, along with our other best friend, Randy Zak, eat lunch

1

together every day at school.

"You can have some of my lunch, if you want, Sabs," I told her as I looked into my own paper bag. As usual, Nooma had packed me a ton of stuff. Nooma is the name my family calls my grandmother. We're Native American Chippewa Indian, and Nooma comes from the Chippewa word for "grandmother." She and my grandfather live with my family, and she always packs lunch for my little brother and me. Today I had a tuna sandwich on homemade whole-wheat bread, pasta salad, carrot sticks, an apple, and some freshly baked chocolate-chip cookies.

"I'll never be able to eat all this myself," I said, passing Sabrina half of my sandwich, some carrot sticks, and a couple of cookies. "I try to tell Nooma she packs too much for me, but she never listens."

"Thanks a lot, Allison," said Sabs. She smiled, and her hazel eyes shone.

Just then I noticed Randy come into the cafeteria. She was wearing an oversize blue-and-black-plaid man's jacket over her one-piece black stretchy jumpsuit, which she calls a catsuit. Randy's from New York City, and I guess you could say she's on the cutting edge of fashion. I really love the way she dresses.

"Oooooh . . . oooooh . . . yeah," Randy sang out as she walked toward us, bopping to the beat of the music coming over her Walkman. "Oooooh . . . yeah . . . yeah," Randy crooned as she approached, snapping her fingers and doing a little spin when she arrived at our table.

"Hi, guys," she said, grinning, as she took off her earphones.

"Hi, Randy," I said, scooting over to make room for her on the bench next to me.

"Wow, Randy, that must have been some song you were listening to," noted Sabrina. "You seemed really into it."

"Huh?" said Randy, looking around. She pulled her Walkman out of her jacket pocket and glanced at the tape. "Oh, yeah, that. Nothing really special."

"So, then, what's all the dancing and singing about?" I asked, pulling my long black ponytail a little tighter. "I mean, if it's not the tape that's putting the pep in your step, it must be something else."

"Correct as usual, Allison Cloud," Randy answered, running her hand through her spiky black hair. "I'm in an totally great mood."

"What are you so happy about, Randy?" asked Katie.

"It must be something pretty good," said Sabs.

"Definitely," I added. "You look like a cat that just found the key to a birdcage."

"Actually, you guys already know about it," said Randy.

"We do?" said Sabs, wrinkling her nose.

"Yeah," replied Randy happily. "I'm just celebrating the fact that last period is canceled today."

"But, Randy, it's not like we all get to go home early or anything," Sabs pointed out. "I mean, we all still have to stay and take that physical test, or whatever it's called."

"National Fitness Exam," I told her. That morning during homeroom, our school principal, Mr. Hansen, had announced that all seventh graders would be taking the National Fitness Exam during last period. "It's supposed to show how well the kids here at Bradley do in physical fitness compared to other seventh graders in the country," I explained.

"Well, whatever it is, it'll definitely be better

than math class with Miss Munson," said Randy. She made a face. "Ugh, Monster Munson."

"The Fitness Exam is probably a good idea for all of us to take anyway," said Katie.

"Definitely," I agreed. "I just read this article in the newspaper the other day about how out of shape American kids are these days. Did you know that nearly one third of American kids are overweight, and that over half don't get enough exercise?"

"None of us are like that, though," said Sabrina. "I mean, I guess maybe I could lose a pound or two —"

"Sabs, you look perfect the way you are," said Randy.

"Definitely," I agreed. Sabrina's always trying the latest fad diet. Luckily, she never sticks to a single one. "I'm sure none of us will have any problem with this fitness test," I added.

"Yeah," said Randy. "We all look like we're in pretty good shape to me — especially you, Katie, Miss Hockey Player."

Katie is the only girl on Bradley's ice hockey team. She spends a lot of time at practice, and she's in really good shape.

"Not to mention you, Allison," Sabrina put

in. "I mean, you're obviously the furthest thing from overweight."

"Really, Al, you're as thin as a stick," said Randy. "You don't have anything to worry about."

I've always been one of those people who can eat as much as they want without gaining weight. In fact, my grandmother's always telling me to put some more meat on my bones — probably because it was considered normal to be a little heavy back in the days when she was younger. I guess that's why she packs me these huge lunches, and why she's always heaping extra food on my plate at dinner.

It was getting late, so we figured we'd better finish our lunch. When the bell rang, we all gathered up our things and got ready for the next period.

The rest of the day went pretty quickly, and before I knew it, it was last period. Randy, Katie, Sabs, and I changed into our Bradley orange sweatshirts and black sweatpants and headed into the girls' gym with the rest of the seventh-grade girls. The boys would be taking the test in their own gym on the other side of the building.

We all sat on mats on the gym floor as Miss Pitts, the head of the girls' phys ed department, stood in front of us with a clipboard in her hand.

She gave a short toot on the whistle that hung around her neck. "All right, girls," she began, "I would like you all to listen carefully. As you know, you're going to be taking the National Fitness Exam today. This test is designed to measure the physical fitness levels of young people all over the country."

I looked around at all the girls in their identical gym shorts and T-shirts. Some kids looked a little nervous, and a few, like Katie, actually looked a little excited.

First Miss Pitts led us through a few stretches. Then we did some jumping jacks to warm up.

"All right," she said, blowing her whistle again for us to stop. "We will now begin the test. All I ask of each of you is that you do your best."

I had to admit, I was already a little out of breath. I glanced over at Katie, Randy, and Sabrina. They looked a little flushed, but they weren't panting like I was. No one was, except for Marnie Hooper. Marnie, who was standing in the row ahead of me, is the heaviest girl in the seventh grade. Even from behind I could see her shoulders heaving.

"For these first few tests," Miss Pitts was saying, "you will need to split up into pairs."

Right away Randy and I looked at each other. We knew without saying anything that the two of us would be partners. And I saw Sabrina edge closer to Katie so they could be partners, too.

"The first test," Miss Pitts went on, "will be to do as many push-ups as you can in one minute."

She showed us the kind of bent-knee push-ups she wanted us to do.

"These are modified push-ups. They're sometimes called 'girls' push-ups,'" she explained. "They're less of a strain on the upper body. Many girls find push-ups difficult to do, because girls aren't born with the same kind of natural upper-body strength as boys. But many girls have more natural lower-body strength, in the hips and legs, than boys."

"No fair," whispered Sabs. "We should get to do 'leg-ups' or something instead."

"I will blow the whistle to signal when timing has begun," Miss Pitts said, "and then again when one minute is over. Whichever partner is not doing the push-ups should count for the other. Then you can switch places."

"I guess I'll go first, Al," Randy volunteered, lying down on the mat and placing her hands on the floor beneath her shoulders.

"All right," Miss Pitts called out, holding up her stopwatch and blowing on her whistle. "Begin!"

I watched and counted as Randy did her push-ups. By the time the whistle blew again, she had done twenty-three of them.

As Miss Pitts moved down the line asking us all for our partners' scores, I realized that Randy had done really well. A lot of the other girls had done only ten or so. In fact, only Katie, who had done twenty-five, had scored higher than Randy.

"Wow, Randy," I said. "I'm impressed."

She shrugged.

"I guess it's all that practicing on the drums," she said. "It really builds up your arms and shoulders." Randy is the drummer in a band called Iron Wombat.

Now it was my turn. I took my place on the mat, and Miss Pitts blew the whistle for us to begin.

At first I thought I was doing pretty well. I did the first two push-ups with no trouble at all. But suddenly, on the third one, my arms began to shake. I tried to stop them, but I couldn't seem to control them. By the fourth push-up, I was moving incredibly slowly. The muscles in my upper arms were really trembling, and all I wanted to do was lie back down on the floor. What was going on? I wondered. Was I doing something wrong? It hadn't looked this tough when Randy was doing it, that was for sure.

By the time I started the fifth push-up, I knew I was never going to be able to finish it. I pushed with all my might, but I couldn't seem to get my elbows straight.

"Come on, Al, you can do it," I heard Randy whisper above me.

But it was no use. I lay back down on the floor, thinking that maybe if I started over, I would be able to regain some of my strength. But once I was lying down, I couldn't seem to make myself move again. The next thing I knew, Miss Pitts was blowing the whistle.

I got myself up off the floor and looked at Randy, who had a sympathetic expression on her face.

"Boy, I really bombed at that," I said.

"Don't worry about it, Al," she replied. "Remember, Miss Pitts said that push-ups are kind of hard for girls."

I knew Randy was just trying to make me feel better, but I was still kind of upset. Especially when I realized that my score of four had been the second lowest in the class — only Marnie Hooper had done worse, with three.

But I couldn't really dwell on it for long, because Miss Pitts was announcing the next test. This time, we were supposed to do as many sit-ups as possible in a minute.

Randy did really well again, but Katie blew everybody away. I was beginning to realize how incredibly fit Katie was.

When it was my turn, I was determined to do better than I had on the push-ups. Maybe Miss Pitts was right about that upper-body-strength stuff and girls.

I lay down on the mat and bent my knees. Randy winked at me and looked encouraging as she sat down and held on to my ankles.

Miss Pitts blew her whistle, and we began. I managed the first few sit-ups without much of a problem, but then I began to feel a terrible strain in my stomach with each one. I could really feel myself slowing down, but this time I was determined not to give up. By this point each sit-up was definitely a huge struggle for me, but I kept at it.

Then, suddenly, I heard the whistle.

"That was better, Al," said Randy. "You did nine."

I sighed. True, maybe I had done slightly better on the sit-ups than I had on the push-ups, but it still wasn't a very good score. Especially compared with the other scores in the class. I was ready to quit right then. I felt incredibly humiliated, and my whole body was aching. But Miss Pitts was already announcing the next test.

"This time you'll be doing as many squat thrusts as you can in one minute," she said.

When it was my turn, my body throbbed with each squat thrust. I was just relieved when the second whistle blew and I could stop.

I was so embarrassed by my score. It was the lowest in the class, lower even than Marnie

Hooper's. The fact that Randy tried to report my score in the quietest voice she could only made me feel worse.

Then Miss Pitts announced that we should all go to the ropes at the far side of the gym.

"All right, girls," she said, "the object of this test is to climb the rope to the ceiling in as little time as possible. There will be a thirty-second time limit."

I joined one of the lines forming in front of the ropes and waited. I was beginning to have this really terrible feeling inside, like a big, tight lump rising in my throat. I swallowed and took a deep breath.

Sabrina and Katie were in the first group, and I watched as they each took a place by a rope. Miss Pitts blew the whistle, and they began climbing.

As I expected, Katie climbed quickly and easily toward the ceiling. But the real surprise was Sabrina, who scampered up to the top of the rope in seconds. It was obvious that Sabs was the fastest climber in the class, and I could tell she was really happy, because she was smiling and there were two bright pink spots on her cheeks as she climbed back down. I had to admit, even though I was feeling pretty bad about myself right then, I was still really proud of Sabs.

The last group moved forward, and I took my place at the bottom of one of the thick, scratchy ropes. I looked up at the gym ceiling, which suddenly seemed incredibly far away. I really didn't want to be doing this. I was completely exhausted, and all my muscles were aching.

But there was no time to think about it, because just then the whistle blew. I reached as high as I could and grabbed on to the rope with my hands. Wrapping my feet around the bottom of the rope, the way I had seen the others do, I tried to pull my body upward.

But it was no use. The muscles in my arms were just too worn out. I felt like I didn't have a drop of energy left in my entire body. I pulled and pulled, but I couldn't seem to get anywhere. Every time I made it a tiny little way up the rope, I would slip back down again. My hands had slid along the rope so many times that my palms were starting to get raw.

I watched as the girls on either side of me made their way up their ropes. It seemed like everyone else was way above me. How were they doing it?

When the whistle blew, all I could feel was incredible relief. I never wanted to see one of those ropes again.

Just then Sabrina came rushing over to me.

"Wow, I thought that was so much fun!" she gushed excitedly. "I mean, I could take or leave that sit-up stuff, but I really love rope-climbing. It makes me feel like when I was a little kid in the school playground."

I looked at her. Obviously she hadn't seen my total failure of an attempt at rope-climbing. I could see that she was really having a good time. Suddenly I felt completely alone. That old lump in my throat appeared again, but I tried not to look too upset.

Then Miss Pitts began to announce the final test. Thank goodness, I thought. All I wanted was for this whole thing to be over.

"For this test," Miss Pitts was saying, "we will be using the indoor track that runs around the gym. The object is to run a mile in twelve minutes or less. One mile is equivalent to twelve laps around our track."

As we filed out the doors of the gym and

took our positions on the track, I sighed. The way I was feeling right then, I wondered if I'd even be able to make it around one lap, let alone twelve!

As Randy took her place next to me, I could tell she was trying to think of something to say that might make me feel better. But suddenly I felt like I couldn't look anyone in the face, not even her.

Miss Pitts blew the whistle, and we all took off. Katie shot quickly ahead of everyone else, with Randy and a group of other girls not too far behind. Already I could feel myself dropping back. Suddenly all I wanted was to be out of there. I wished I had never had to take this test, that I could be home talking to my mother or watching my grandmother cooking in the kitchen.

As more and more people passed me, I got more and more upset about the whole thing. This test had been one of the most humiliating experiences I had ever had, and I felt like I was about to burst into tears. I blinked my eyes and tried to think about something else. I imagined playing with my brother, Charlie, in his treehouse; holding my baby sister, Barrett, on my lap; and sitting in my room with a good book. But all those thoughts did was make me feel more like crying.

With each lap, the crowd of runners became thinner and thinner. Girls were completing their twelve laps and leaving the track. Soon Katie, Randy, and Sabs were nowhere in sight. By the time Miss Pitts blew the twelve-minute whistle, Marnie Hooper and I were the only ones left.

As I left the track, I felt a horrible cramp in my side. I was completely out of breath. I knew Randy, Sabrina, and Katie were probably waiting for me in the locker room, but all I wanted was to get home. How could I face anyone after all that talking I had done at lunch about how out of shape American kids were — especially now that I knew I was one of them!

# Chapter Two

*Randy calls Allison.*

MRS.
CLOUD: Hello?

RANDY: Hi, Mrs. Cloud, this is Randy. Is Allison there?

MRS.
CLOUD: Why, yes, Randy. I'll go get her for you.

RANDY: Thanks.

ALLISON: Hello?

RANDY: Hi, Al, it's me.

ALLISON: Oh, hi, Randy.

RANDY: Listen, I just called to see if you're okay — I mean, we all waited for you after the test today, but I guess we missed you or something.

ALLISON: Yeah, well, I guess I wasn't really in the mood to talk to anybody.

18

I'm sorry I kept you guys waiting, though.

RANDY: Don't worry about it, Al. It's just that I was a little worried about you.

ALLISON: Well, I guess I was kind of upset. I can't believe I failed the Fitness Exam. The only thing I managed to do right in that stupid test this afternoon was to show everybody in the class how totally out of shape I am.

RANDY: Oh, Al, come on, no one was even paying attention to anyone else's scores. So you're not in perfect shape. You have nothing to worry about — you look great.

ALLISON: Well, I don't feel great. I was really embarrassed today.

RANDY: Well, then, what are you going to do about it, Al?

ALLISON: I don't know, Randy. The last thing I feel like doing after today's disaster is more exercise. Maybe I'm just not the athletic type.

RANDY: Well, if it upset you that much, you

should think about getting into some kind of exercise program.

ALLISON: Yeah, well, maybe you're right. Maybe I should just accept it — some people should just stick to books and stuff.

RANDY: Well, no one's saying you have to become an Olympic track-and-field star or anything, Al. But having a physical hobby can be a lot of fun. And sometimes the physical stuff can actually help you feel better mentally, too. I know when I'm really upset, there are times when nothing but my skateboard can make me feel better.

ALLISON: Well, I guess I'll think about it. Right now I have to go, though. My grandmother's calling us all for dinner.

RANDY: Okay, bye, Al.

ALLISON: Bye, Ran. And Randy?

RANDY: Yeah?

ALLISON: Thanks for calling.

RANDY: Sure, no problem. See you in school tomorrow. *Ciao.*

*Randy calls Sabrina.*

SAM:        Hello?

RANDY:      Hi, Sam, it's Randy. Is Sabrina there?

SAM:        Hi, Randy. Sure, she's here, hang on. SABS! S-A-A-B-S! S-A-A-A-A-A-B-S!

RANDY:      Yow, Sam, you don't have to scream in my ear!

SAM:        Here she comes.

SABRINA:    Hello?

RANDY:      Hi, Sabs, it's me, Randy.

SABRINA:    Oh, hi, Randy. What's up?

RANDY:      Well, I just got off the phone with Allison.

SABRINA:    Did she tell you what happened to her today? I mean, it was like she just disappeared after gym.

RANDY:      Well, she was pretty upset about the way the Fitness Exam went today.

SABRINA:    Oh, Randy, that's terrible. I wonder what we can do to make her feel better.

RANDY:      Well, that's kind of the problem.

Allison's got to be the one to help herself feel better this time. I suggested that she get involved in some kind of exercise.

SABRINA: Hey, that's a great idea. You know, I've been working out with these exercise videos lately. I think they're really starting to make a difference. Now when I run up the stairs to my room I don't get out of breath the way I used to. Maybe Allison should start doing some kind of exercise — I'm sure she'd feel a lot better.

RANDY: Yeah, well, I tried telling her that, but she didn't really take it very well. It's like the whole experience of the Fitness Exam has turned her off the idea of exercise completely. She keeps saying she's not the athletic type.

SABRINA: Hey, Katie's the athletic one. Maybe she'll know how to get Al out of her slump.

RANDY: That's a good idea, Sabs. I think I'll give Katie a call right now and see what she says.

SABRINA: Okay, bye, Randy.

RANDY: *Ciao.*

*Randy calls Katie.*

KATIE: Hello?

RANDY: Hi, Katie, it's Randy. Listen, I kind of wanted to talk to you about Allison.

KATIE: Oh, yeah, what happened to her today? Is Al okay?

RANDY: Well, she was pretty upset about not doing well in that Fitness Exam.

KATIE: I noticed she wasn't doing too well. She must be really upset, especially after our talk at lunch.

RANDY: Well, I suggested she might feel better if she got into some kind of exercise program.

KATIE: Good idea, Randy. Allison's problem is that she's never really had to exercise, because she's naturally thin.

RANDY: Well, now her problem is that the whole Fitness Exam experience

23

has kind of turned her off to exercise.

KATIE: I can understand that. Besides, push-ups and sit-ups aren't exactly the most inspiring form of exercise.

RANDY: Well, they're not like skateboarding, which is at least fun.

KATIE: Right, or like sports, where there's the excitement of the competition to keep you going. All Allison needs to do is find the kind of exercise that's right for her.

RANDY: That's going to be pretty hard if she's not even looking.

KATIE: Well, maybe we can get her to give it a chance somehow. You know, help her get started.

RANDY: Great idea, Katie. But how do we do it?

KATIE: Well, we could start by introducing her to the kinds of exercise we like best.

RANDY: That sounds good. Al's bound to have a good time if she's doing something with her friends.

KATIE:    We have to be really careful, though. We don't want to hurt her feelings or be too obvious about it. Probably the best idea is for each of us to quietly invite Allison to do something active.

RANDY:    Good thinking, Katie. And I agree, we have to be totally cool about it.

KATIE:    If we can get Allison rolling with some kind of exercise program, she can take it from there.

RANDY:    Katie, I think you just gave me an idea. Listen, I'm going to call Sabs and tell her about our plan, and then I have some planning of my own to do. I'll see you tomorrow.

KATIE:    Okay, Randy, bye.

RANDY:    *Ciao.*

*Randy calls Sabrina.*

SABRINA:    Hello?

RANDY:    Hi, Sabs, it's me, Randy, again. I just got off the phone with Katie, and I think she had a really good idea.

SABRINA:    Great! What is it?

25

RANDY: Well, Katie thinks that Allison's bound to find some form of exercise she can really get into. The problem is that she's not looking. So, according to Katie, it's up to us, her friends, to help her find it. And I think I may have an idea already, but first I need to talk to Sam.

SABRINA: My brother? Why?

RANDY: I'll need his help if my plan's going to work. Just trust me.

SABRINA: Okay, but it doesn't make much sense to me. I'll get him. SAM! S-A-A-M! S-A-A-A-A-A-M!!!

RANDY: Yow, my ear! (*muttering to herself*) Some things definitely run in families.

SAM: Hello?

RANDY: Hey, Sam, it's Randy. Listen, I need to ask you a favor.

SAM: Sure, Randy, what is it?

RANDY: I need to borrow your skateboard for a day or two.

SAM: My skateboard? Why? Is something wrong with yours?

RANDY:     Listen, Sam, I can't explain, but I promise I'll take good care of it.

SAM:       Well, okay, Randy, but only because it's you.

RANDY:     Great, Sam, I'll get it from you in school tomorrow, okay?

SAM:       Sure thing, Randy. See you tomorrow.

RANDY:     Bye, Sam, and thanks.

# Chapter Three

The next morning when I got to school, I found Randy standing in front of my locker. She had on a pair of black-and-red-checked leggings with an oversize black sweatshirt, and her black leather jacket was slung over one shoulder.

"Hi, Al," she said cheerfully.

"Hi, Randy," I answered, putting my purple canvas bookbag down on the ground and reaching around her to open my locker.

"Listen, Al, I was thinking. What do you say we go over to Pizza Palace today after school?" Randy asked.

"That sounds okay," I answered. "But I thought you liked going to Fitzie's better." Fitzie's is the Bradley hangout. They make great french fries and really thick shakes, and Randy's always saying how cool it is because it's like a fifties diner. She says it's hip without even trying to be. "Besides," I added, "Pizza

28

Palace is all the way over on Market Street, and Fitzie's is just down the street."

"Yeah, well, we always go to Fitzie's," said Randy. "Maybe we need a change of pace. Besides, I've had kind of a craving for a pepperoni slice lately."

"Sounds good to me," I said, tucking my black-and-white-striped turtleneck into my black miniskirt and adjusting my matching black-and-white-striped stretch headband.

Just then Sabrina walked up to us. She was wearing a long-sleeved white cotton T-shirt with little pink rosebuds on it, a man's gray vest, a pair of worn-in jeans, and pink high-tops. Her curly hair was pulled into a knot on top of her head and held in place with a white scrunchy.

"Hi, guys," she said, greeting us.

"Hey, Sabs, nice sneakers," said Randy.

"Really," I added, "you look so cute today."

"Thanks," replied Sabs. "The vest is really my dad's. I got the idea from an article in *Young Chic* called "The Shirt off His Back — How to Raid a Guy's Closet with a Feminine Touch.""

"Well, you've definitely got a lot of closets to raid at your house, Sabs," I said. Sabrina has four brothers. Three of them are older than she is, and one of them, Sam, is her twin. Sam's technically older than Sabrina, too — only by four minutes, but he never lets her forget it.

"You know, speaking of my house, Allison," said Sabs, glancing at Randy, "I was thinking, maybe you could come over today after school."

"Actually, Sabs," Randy put in quickly, "Al's probably going to go over to Market Street with me after school today."

"Randy and I were just going to go have some pizza," I added. "Why don't you come, too, Sabs?"

"No, no, that's okay," she said, eyeing Randy. "Maybe you can come over tomorrow instead, Allison."

"I don't see why we can't all just do something together today," I said. I looked down the hall and saw Katie heading toward us. She was wearing a white scooped-neck top with a short, flared gray skirt and a gray-and-white polka-dot ribbon in her hair. "There's Katie. We can ask her, too."

"No," said Randy quickly. "I mean, I'm pretty sure Katie's busy this afternoon." She shot a look at Sabs. "Right, Sabs?"

"Oh, yes, that's right," said Sabrina. "Katie has hockey practice or something."

"Are you sure?" I asked. "I mean, I thought hockey practice wasn't until the day after tomorrow."

"No, no, I'm pretty sure Katie's busy today," Randy said again.

I looked at her. Suddenly it seemed to me like she and Sabs were acting really strange.

"Well, anyway, here's Katie now," I said as Katie drew near us. "So we might as well ask her ourselves."

"Ask me what?" said Katie.

"If you're free after sch —" I began.

"Sabs and I were just explaining to Allison that you couldn't possibly do anything today after school," said Randy quickly, cutting me off.

"That's right," added Sabrina. "We were just talking about how you have hockey practice or something."

Katie looked confused.

"What are you talking about?" she began. "I don't ha —"

"Katie, I think maybe you're forgetting your

own schedule," said Randy firmly.

"That's right," said Sabs, looking at Katie. "You and I are both busy today after school, Katie, so I guess Allison's just going to have to spend some time with Randy alone."

"Ooohhh!" said Katie suddenly. "I get it — I mean, I remember, I do have something to do after school today."

"That's right," repeated Sabrina, "and so do I. So I guess it'll just be you two."

"Wait a minute, Sabs," I said. "Why did you invite me over to your house after school today if you already had something to do?"

"Oh, did I invite you over for today?" asked Sabs. "I guess I made a mistake. I guess I meant to invite you over tomorrow after school."

"Are you sure?" I asked. There was definitely something very strange going on in this whole conversation, but I couldn't put my finger on it.

"Really, Al," said Sabs, nodding her head up and down.

"Okay," I said, still a little confused. Still, the whole thing seemed very strange to me. Something about my entire conversation with Katie, Randy, and Sabs just didn't make sense.

But just then the bell rang for first period. We all hurried to get our things together and get to our classes, and I pretty much forgot all about it.

After school, Randy and I headed over to Market Street so we could go to Pizza Palace as planned. As we were walking, I suddenly realized that she had two skateboards tucked under her arm. At first I hadn't noticed anything peculiar, because Randy usually takes her skateboard everywhere with her anyway. But this time, in addition to her own plain black skateboard — Randy always likes black — she was carrying a bright orange one.

"Hey, Randy, what's with the two skateboards?" I asked. "Don't tell me you've been using one for each foot!" I laughed. "I mean, wouldn't it just be easier to get a pair of roller skates or something?"

Randy glanced at me out of the corner of her eye.

"Actually, Al," she said, "I kind of thought that maybe you might like to try it. You know, before our pizza."

"What?" I asked, amazed. "Me? But I've never been on a skateboard in my life."

"Well, there's a first time for everything, right?" said Randy. "We can try some really simple stuff. There's a great parking lot in back of Pizza Palace. They just put new tar on it, and no one ever uses it. It's perfect."

I looked at her.

"Randy, that's why you wanted to go to Pizza Palace, isn't it?" I asked. "You had this idea in mind the whole time."

Randy looked a little sheepish.

"Well, I guess you're right, Al," she replied. "I was hoping that maybe you would give it a try."

"I don't know, Randy," I said. "Somehow skateboarding just doesn't seem like me."

"Just give it a try, Al. I'll help you," said Randy. "Look, here we are now."

Randy led me around to the back of Pizza Palace. The parking lot was newly tarred, smooth, and completely empty, just like she had promised.

"See, it's like our own private little training area," observed Randy, putting her khaki knapsack on the ground, stepping onto her skateboard, and rolling the orange one over to where I was standing.

I looked around. There was no one in sight. The back of Pizza Palace didn't have any windows. It made me feel a little better to think that no one could see us.

"Now, what you want to remember, Al, is to keep your weight forward," she said, gliding by. "If you lean too far backward, the board can slip out from under you. And you don't have enough padding where it counts for that."

I giggled nervously. I had to admit, Randy did make it look kind of fun.

"Also, you want to keep your knees bent," Randy went on, skating around me in circles. "If your legs are too stiff, you lose the flow of the movement."

"It sure seems like a lot of things to think about," I said, giving the orange skateboard a little push with my toe.

"Well, maybe at first," said Randy. "But after a while it just sort of all comes together, and you don't really have to think about what you're doing that much anymore." She did a little twirl on the back two wheels of her skateboard.

"All right," I said, taking a deep breath and looking down at the orange skateboard nervously. "What do I do?"

"Just put one foot on it and push off gently with the other foot," instructed Randy, who had somehow managed to make her skateboard jump up onto a curb at the edge of the parking lot.

Carefully, I put one foot down on the skateboard. But then, as I went to push off with the other one, the board went scooting out and away from me.

"Oh, let's just forget it, Randy. I can't do this."

"No one can the first time they try. It takes practice. Here, I have an idea. Why don't you stand on the board with both feet, and I'll just pull you around a little. That way you can kind of get the feel of it."

"All right," I said as Randy retrieved my board. "But not too fast, okay?"

"I promise."

So I put first one foot and then the other up on the skateboard. Then Randy took hold of my hands and slowly began to pull. At first I felt a little wobbly, but then I relaxed and kind of got my balance.

"Okay, now keep your knees a little bent," Randy coached. "That's it."

As Randy pulled me around the parking lot, I discovered that I could control the direction of the skateboard just by shifting my weight a little from side to side.

"All right! You're doing really well, Al!" said Randy happily. "Now let's see if you can get it going under your own steam. Try pushing off the ground with one foot."

After a few shaky starts, I managed to push off with one foot and glide a few feet.

"Allison, you're doing it!" Randy cried enthusiastically.

Slowly I made my way around, with Randy zipping by me, twisting and turning and doing all kinds of impossible-looking stunts.

"Isn't it the greatest?" she called out, making her board leap off the ground and turn around in midair.

I didn't know what to say. Sure, I had kind of gotten the hang of it, but somehow it seemed kind of pointless just skating around a parking lot like this.

"I don't know, Randy," I said as I slowly glided by her.

"Just wait, Al. If you really practice all the time, you'll be ready to learn some tricks and stuff. That's when it really gets fun."

I completed another circle and carefully jumped off the board.

"Randy," I said, picking it up and heading toward where she was skating in tiny circles on the back wheels of her board, "I have to be honest with you. I don't know if I could ever really get into this enough to want to practice all the time like that."

Randy's face fell.

"You mean you don't like it?" she asked, amazed.

"It's okay," I said. "I mean, thanks for teaching me and everything, but somehow I just can't see myself getting totally into it. You know, buying a skateboard of my own and all that."

Randy jumped off her board, flipping it into the air and catching it with one hand.

"Yeah, well, I guess I just sort of fell in love with it right away," she said, grinning. "Maybe it's not for everybody."

"Thanks for letting me try, though."

"Sure, Al."

"Hey," I said, "how about if we go inside now and get that pepperoni slice?"

"Definitely," agreed Randy. "I'm starved."

It made me feel really good that Randy understood. I know how totally into skateboarding she is, and I was glad she wasn't disappointed that I didn't feel the same way about it. That's one of the great things about being best friends with her. Even though we sometimes seem like we're really different on the outside, we pretty much always understand each other on the inside. But that's why the more I thought about it, the less I understood how come Randy had brought me skateboarding in the first place. She hadn't even asked me about it!

# Chapter Four

The next day after school, Sabrina and I walked into her kitchen and put our bookbags down on the table.

"Listen, Sabs," I began, pulling my notebook out of my bag, "I've been thinking. The first thing we should probably do is to make a list of all the events and dates we're supposed to know. Then, afterward, we can test each other on them."

"What are you talking about, Allison?" asked Sabs, wriggling out of her dark green corduroy jacket and tossing it on the back of a kitchen chair.

"The social studies test, of course," I said, surprised. "Isn't that why you invited me over?"

"Oh, that," said Sabrina. "Well, yes, I guess so — partly."

"Partly?" I repeated, confused. "What do

you mean?"

"Oh, I don't know," Sabs answered, casually tossing her wavy auburn hair over her shoulder. "I mean, sure, we can study for the test if you want, but I thought maybe we could do a bunch of stuff."

I looked at her. After all, wasn't she the one who had suggested this study session in the first place?

"What else did you have in mind, Sabs?" I asked her.

"Well, I think we should start with a little snack to boost our energy," she answered, opening the refrigerator.

"Sounds great," I said. "I'm starved."

"How about an apple?" offered Sabs, taking out a bowl of fruit.

"Sure, thanks," I said, taking the one she handed me.

Just then, Sam, Sabrina's twin brother, and Luke, one of her older brothers, came bounding through the kitchen.

"Hi, Sabs. Hi Al," said Sam.

"Hey, Sabs, where did Mom say those brownies were?" asked Luke, opening and shutting a few cabinets.

"I found them!" cried Sam, peeling back the foil from a plate on the counter.

"Excellent!" said Luke, grabbing a handful. "Homemade brownies."

"Hey, don't hog them all, Luke!" yelled Sam, grabbing a few for himself. "See you later, Sabs. Bye, Al. We're going to shoot a few hoops outside."

I looked at Sabs as her two brothers banged out the back door.

"Sabrina, do you mean to tell me that we're eating apples when there are homemade brownies around?" I asked her, amazed. I had never known Sabs to pass up anything chocolate.

"Well, maybe we can have some brownies later," she replied. "I just thought we shouldn't eat anything too heavy right now." She laughed. "I mean, you know what they say about studying on a full stomach."

"Huh?" I said. What was she talking about? I had never heard anyone say anything about studying on a full stomach.

"Well, I guess we'd better get this over with — I mean, get started," said Sabrina, pulling a notebook out of her bag and sitting down at the kitchen table. "Now, what was it you said we should do, Allison?"

We began making a list of all the important dates we would need to know for the test. But I couldn't help noticing that Sabrina's mind seemed to be somewhere else. I was beginning to wonder why she had invited me over in the first place.

Twenty minutes later she stood up from her chair and stretched.

"Well, I think it's time for a break," she announced.

"Okay," I agreed. We hadn't really been getting much work done, anyway.

"I have an idea," said Sabs. "Let's go into the den and watch some TV or something."

"Sounds good to me," I said. "What's on?"

"Oh, I don't know," she replied as we walked out of the kitchen, "but I'm sure we'll find something."

I followed her into the den and flopped down on the big blue couch across from the TV.

Sabrina picked up the remote control, turned on the TV, and began flipping quickly through the channels.

"Oh, well, I guess there's nothing good on,"

she said. "Maybe we should watch a video."

"But, Sabs, you were changing the channels so quickly, how could you even tell what was on?" I asked her.

"Oh, there's never really anything good on at this time," she answered, heading over to the TV and flipping open the video cabinet underneath it. "We've got some really cool new videos, though."

She reached into the cabinet, pulled out a video, and slipped it into the VCR.

"This is a really neat tape," she said as five women in leotards, tights, and sneakers appeared on the screen. "It's aerobics."

Some dance music with a pretty heavy beat began to play, and the woman in the front began to lead the four in back of her in a series of exercises.

"It's really fun," said Sabs, tapping her foot in time to the music. "Want to try it with me?"

"All right," I replied, shrugging, "if you really want to."

I got up from the couch and stood next to Sabrina. The women on TV stretched their arms above their heads in time to the music, and we copied them. Then they put their arms on their shoulders and twisted from side to side. Whatever they did, Sabs and I followed along.

Before long, my mind began to wander. There was something about the beat of the music that made my brain feel sort of numb. It wasn't that it was bad to listen to. It was just that it never changed. It was kind of like listening to someone bang the same rhythm out on a drum over and over again. And we did the same movements over and over, too. There wasn't a whole lot to keep my interest. Before I knew it, I wasn't really paying attention.

Suddenly Sabrina interrupted my thoughts.

"Allison, kick the other leg," she said. "They finished on that side — it's time to switch."

"Oh," I said, changing my kicks to the other leg and trying to focus on what was happening on the screen in front of me.

"Hey, Sabs, how long is this thing?" I asked as we continued kicking.

"About twenty minutes more," she answered, her cheeks flushed. "Why? Aren't you having fun?"

"Well, it's okay, I guess," I said. "But to tell you the truth, I'm kind of bored. Maybe if I could read or something while I was doing it, I might like it a little more."

"Gee, I'm sorry, Allison," said Sabs, stopping her kicks. "I mean, I was sure you were going to love this."

"Well, I guess it's just not for me," I said. "But you go ahead and finish if you want to."

"Nah," she said, walking over to the VCR and turning it off. "Let's go see if Luke and Sam left us any of those brownies."

We went back into the kitchen, where we helped ourselves to the last two brownies on the plate and washed them down with a tall glass of cold milk. And after we were done, I actually managed to get Sabs to do some real studying with me for that test.

Later, as I was walking home from Sabrina's, I couldn't stop thinking about that aerobics tape. It seemed kind of funny that Sabs had suddenly put it on like that. It was just like the way Randy had suddenly wanted to teach me to skateboard.

Then I realized it was no coincidence that both Randy and Sabrina had invited me to do something physical with them! I knew exactly what my friends were up to. And although I kept telling myself that they thought they were trying to help me, I couldn't help being mad at them. The more I thought about it, the madder I got. I wondered when Katie would try to get me to go ice-skating with her. Whenever that was, I would be ready for her!

The next morning in school, Sabs, Katie, Randy, and I were putting our things away in our lockers. Suddenly Katie looked at me and cleared her throat. Here goes, I told myself.

"Listen, Allison, I was thinking," she began, fidgeting with one of the white buttons on her pale yellow cardigan. "Maybe you and I could do something today after school."

"That sounds nice, Katie," I replied, hanging my navy-blue quilted jacket in my locker and trying not to show how angry I was. "What did you have in mind?"

"Well, I have hockey practice right after school," she said. "But maybe you could meet me at the rink when it's over."

I looked at the three of them. Katie was still playing with her button, and Sabrina and Randy were suddenly very busy rummaging around in their lockers.

"Hmmm," I said loudly, "why do I get the feeling that when I show up at the rink today, there will just happen to be an extra pair of skates my size there?"

Katie's face turned pink.

Randy's head popped out of her locker.

"Ooops," she said.

"Oh, Allison," said Katie, biting her lower lip. "We're sorry."

"Really," added Sabs, looking at me. "Were we that obvious?"

"I hope you're not mad at us," Katie said, looking down at her black suede flats.

"Well, I am," I said, "even though I know you guys were just trying to help me out."

"You're not really upset, are you, Al?" asked Randy, running her hand through her spiky black hair and sighing.

"Well, I guess I'll get over it. But you have to promise to let me take care of this in my own way."

"Does that mean you're not coming skating with me?" asked Katie.

"Yes," I said. "And I'm not going skateboarding or doing aerobics, either. Maybe there's something out there that'll be fun for me."

"How will you find out, Al?" asked Randy.

I didn't know what to say. Then I suddenly got an idea. I'd really do it my way. I told the girls, "Right after school today I'm heading straight for the library to do some research on the whole thing."

"Wow, leave it to you, Allison," said Sabrina. "I never would have thought of looking up something like that at the library."

"Well, I hope they'll have just what I'm looking for," I told her.

It turned out that the library had more than enough information for me. Mrs. Twersky, the librarian, was very helpful, and by the time I had looked under "Physical Fitness," "Health," "Sports and Athletics," and "Exercise," I had a huge stack of books to check out.

Somehow I made it home, my arms full of books, and struggled up the driveway to our house. I was really excited, and I planned to go straight up to my room and start reading.

The only problem was, I couldn't open the front door to our house with all those books in my arms. I pushed against it, but it wouldn't open unless you turned the handle. Next I tried to turn the handle by sort of sliding my elbow against it, but it didn't work.

"Mom!" I yelled, trying to knock on the door with one of my knees. "Nooma!"

But our front door is really thick and heavy, and I knew my mother and my grandmother could be anywhere in the house. They probably couldn't even hear me.

I decided to try the back door. Usually my grandmother was in the kitchen in the afternoon. I heaved the books higher against my chest and struggled around to the back of the house. I was beginning to feel that just carrying these books home was enough of an exercise program for anyone!

As I slumped against the back door, I could feel the huge pile of books slipping even lower against my body. I had to lift one knee to keep them in place.

"Mom!" I yelled again, feeling the pile slip lower and lower. "Nooma! Anyone! Can somebody open the door, please!"

I leaned against the door to keep the books from dropping any lower. Where was everybody?

Then I heard footsteps. Finally!

Suddenly the door opened and I fell onto the kitchen floor, books scattering everywhere.

"Allison, are you all right?" I heard Nooma ask.

I looked up.

"Hi, everybody," I said and got up and walked over to where my mother was sitting with my baby sister. "Hi, Barrett," I said, giving her a little tickle under the chin. She giggled.

"What's all this, Allison?" asked my mother.

As I picked up the books from the floor, I said, "I've decided to start some kind of exercise program."

"Whatever for?" asked Nooma, looking up from her sewing. "Why, you're as thin as a rail. What you need is to put a little meat on those bones. Did you eat that lunch I packed for you today?"

"Nooma, it would take a sumo wrestler to eat everything that you pack for me every day," I replied. "Besides, I have a good appetite. That's not the problem. In fact, exercising might even 'put some meat on my bones,' by helping me develop some muscle."

"I was never really the athletic type," said my mother. "But your father used to be quite the basketball player when I first met him. I'm sure he'd be happy to take you out and teach

51

you how to play sometime, Allison. Or maybe Mary would take you running." Mary Birdsong is the college student who lives with us and helps take care of my little brother and sister.

"Well, actually, I think I probably need to find something to do on my own," I said. "From what I can tell, you have to pick something to do that you really enjoy. Dad likes basketball — I need to find out what I like. That's why I just took out a whole bunch of books from the library. I plan to research the subject until I find the thing that's right for me."

My mother raised her eyebrows.

"Well, I don't really know that much about it," she said, "but reading seems like a rather unusual way to try a physical activity."

"Well, reading has always helped me figure things out in the past," I countered, "so why shouldn't it now? As a matter of fact, I think I'll go upstairs and start right away."

It took me two trips to get the books up to my room because I also picked up a snack to munch on while I was reading.

I love my room. My parents had it built for me when Barrett was born. It's really special because it has two separate entrances. There are also these really pretty french doors leading to my own private terrace, where there's a white wicker swing. And there are these great ceiling-to-floor windows on three sides of the room. During the day it's almost like being in a tree-house, and when I go to bed, I can see the stars.

I took my snack — a freshly baked banana muffin and a glass of apple juice — and, opening the first book, settled myself into my rocking chair near the french doors.

***

Three weeks later, when the books were due, I still hadn't found my exercise program. I had read about everything from weight lifting to pole vaulting to volleyball, but somehow none of it seemed right. For some things, like skiing, you needed lots of fancy equipment. For others, like tennis, you had to have a partner. And some of them, like jogging, just sounded boring. I felt like I just wasted three whole weeks.

Randy helped me return the books to the library. When we got there, she went to look around, and I waited at the desk to return the books to Mrs. Twersky.

"I hope they were helpful," she said, smiling as she took the books from me and stacked them on the returns cart. She looked so sweet and hopeful that I somehow didn't have the heart to tell her the truth.

"Yes, thank you very much," I answered.

She beamed.

"All the answers are right here at the library," she told me, patting a stack of books on her desk proudly. "You just have to know where to look."

I said good-bye to Mrs. Twersky and found Randy standing in front of the Community Bulletin Board near the front door.

"See anything interesting?" I asked her, looking at all the signs for free kittens and baby-sitting services that people had put up.

"Well, there's this sign over here," she said, pointing. "Somebody selling an electric guitar. Sounds like a pretty good deal, too. I'm going to take the number down and tell the guys in Iron Wombat about it."

I glanced at the fliers advertising cars for sale, pottery classes, and rooms for rent. Suddenly something caught my eye.

TAKE THE PLUNGE
THE ACORN FALLS YWCA OFFERS SWIMMING

SESSIONS AND LESSONS FOR ALL LEVELS. FUN, AND
GOOD FOR YOU, TOO! RECREATIONAL, DIVING,
TEAM SWIMMING, CLUBS, ETC.

CHILDREN * ADULTS * TEENS

"Hey!" I said suddenly. "Look at that —
'Take the Plunge'!"

"Oh, yeah," said Randy. "So, what about it?"

"So, that's what I want to do!" I said excitedly. "I love swimming. At least I always used to. I
haven't really done it in a while."

"Really, Al? Swimming?" said Randy.

"My family used to go to the lake on the
reservation all the time," I told her. "Back when
we used to go visit my grandparents there,
before they moved in with us."

"So you actually know how to swim, then,"
said Randy. "I've always been a terrible swimmer, myself. I guess I really didn't get much of a
chance to practice in New York City, though."

"I definitely loved it," I said, remembering.
"My mother used to have to call and call to get
me out of the water. I haven't really had a
chance to swim that much since my grandparents moved in with us, but I'm sure I still know
how." I looked at Randy. "Wow, I think I've

found it — I think I've found my exercise program."

"That's great, Al," she said. "I'm really happy for you."

"Boy, can you believe it?" I said, sighing. "I mean, after dragging all those books home from the library and reading practically every single word in them, the answer was right here all along! I guess Mrs. Twersky was right."

"Huh?" said Randy.

"Mrs. Twersky, the librarian," I explained. "She was right — all the answers are here at the library if you know where to look!"

# Chapter Five

On Saturday morning I stood in the women's locker room of the Acorn Falls YWCA, changing into my purple one-piece bathing suit. I couldn't help thinking about the last time I had worn it, in the swimsuit competition of the Junior Miss Acorn Falls Pageant, a contest that Sabrina and I had entered a little while ago. Except that time, all I had to do was stroll across the stage, trying to look good. Now I was going to have to swim.

I had to admit I was feeling kind of nervous. Signing up for swimming lessons had seemed like a really good idea when I was with Randy at the library, but now that I was standing in a strange locker room surrounded by strange girls, I wasn't sure.

I had decided to sign up for Girls' Lap Swim, which was supposed to be a basic swimming class for girls twelve to fifteen years old. It met twice a week, on Saturday mornings and Wednesday afternoons after school.

As I was slipping my feet into my blue rubber thongs, a pretty, petite girl with short curly blond hair and freckles pulled open the locker next to mine and threw her stuff in.

"Over here, Melanie!" she called out. "I got us a locker!"

I began struggling to get my long black braid into my white swim cap. Suddenly a second girl, who looked exactly like the first one, appeared. For a moment I thought I was seeing double. In fact, I was so startled that, as I was stretching my cap to fit it over my hair, it snapped out of my hands and flew right against the second girl's leg.

"Oh, gosh, I'm really sorry," I said, feeling my face get warm.

She grinned, her eyes twinkling.

"Don't worry about it," she replied, reaching for the cap and handing it back to me.

"Really," said the first girl, smiling exactly the way the other one had, "these little caps definitely weren't made with long hair like yours in mind."

I smiled back. I realized that these two girls

must be identical twins. I had definitely never seen two people who looked so much alike.

"Yeah, I guess you're right," I said, taking the cap back. "Sometimes having long hair can be kind of a pain."

"Oh, but yours is so pretty," one of them said quickly. "I always wanted perfectly straight hair."

"Really?" I asked, amazed. "I always thought it would be kind of fun to have curls like yours."

"Fun?" she answered, wrinkling her nose. "Well, it's definitely not any fun when it frizzes up from the chlorine in the pool. By the way, my name's Melanie."

"And I'm Stephanie," said the other one.

"Hi," I said. "I'm Allison. Have you guys been swimming here for a long time?"

"A little over a year," Stephanie told me.

"Wow," I said. "I hope I'll be the right level for this class. I haven't been swimming in a pretty long time."

"Oh, I'm sure you'll be fine," said Melanie, pulling up the strap of her red tank suit. I noticed that Stephanie had the identical suit in blue.

"Really," said Stephanie, "we could barely even swim at all when we started a year ago."

I had finally managed to get my bathing cap on. I grabbed my blue goggles, threw my towel over one shoulder, and closed my locker door.

"Which way to the pool?" I asked them.

"Follow us," said Melanie, slipping her feet into her thongs.

"First we have to shower off," explained Stephanie, leading the way. "Then we'll introduce you to David Steele. He's our coach."

Melanie giggled.

"He's always getting the two of us mixed up," she said.

"Well, you do look an awful lot alike," I said.

"That's why I always wear a blue bathing suit and Melanie always wears a red one," explained Stephanie.

After we had rinsed off in the shower, we all walked down a blue-tiled corridor and out into the pool area.

The pool was really big, and it was separated into several lanes by long ropes strung through red plastic floats. A few girls were already swimming in the water, and several more were sitting around on the blue-tile-covered benches. At the far end of the room stood a young dark-haired man in black shorts and a black-and-white-striped shirt. Around his neck was a whistle, and in his hand was a clipboard.

"Come on," said Stephanie. "There's David."

"Hi, David!" Melanie sang out.

The man waved.

"Hi, girls," the man said.

We walked over to him.

"David, this is Allison," said Melanie.

"She's new today," Stephanie explained.

"Ah, yes," he said, looking down at his clipboard, "Allison Cloud." He looked up at me, his dark eyes twinkling. "Welcome. I'm David Steele, the water activities director here at the Y."

"Hi," I said.

"Allison, why don't we start you out in the slow lane over at the end and see how you do," he said, pointing to a lane at the far end of the pool.

"Don't worry," Melanie whispered as we headed toward the pool. "He always puts new kids in the slow lane. He'll probably move you up to a faster lane soon."

That was no problem as far as I was concerned. The slow lane definitely sounded like a good place to start.

Just then David Steele blew his whistle.

"Okay, gang, we're going to begin," he announced. "Everybody grab a kickboard and go to your lane for the first drill."

I followed the rest of the class over to a corner where the red kickboards were piled and took one. Then I walked back to my lane, where one girl was already swimming around with her board and a tall girl in a bright purple bathing suit and matching cap was getting into the water.

"All right, gang," David said in a loud voice. "Everybody in! Now, a brief reminder — we all want to try to swim in the same direction. In this class, that direction is clockwise. That means you should be heading up the left side of your lane and back down the right side. And please remember to be aware of the others in your lane."

I tossed my board into the water and lowered myself down in after it. The two other girls in my lane had already begun, so I waited until there was some space between me and them before I began.

I held the board at arm's length in front of me and started kicking. The water felt cool and smooth against my legs as I glided through it. In a few moments I reached the other end of the pool and turned around to back. As I passed the girl in the purple bathing suit, she smiled at me.

After we had swum several lengths of the pool, I heard David Steele blow his whistle.

"All right, now, let's see that backstroke," he said. I put my board up onto the side of the pool, flipped over onto my back, and began swimming.

The backstroke drill was followed by the breaststroke and the crawl. It felt great to be in the water, and the time went by quickly. A couple of times David stopped by the side of the pool and gave me a few pointers, but generally I thought I was doing really well.

The next thing I knew, David was blowing the whistle for the end of class. I couldn't believe an hour had gone by already! David said he had an announcement to make to all of us before we left, so I climbed out of the pool with the others and picked up my towel.

"Great class, huh?" said the tall girl in the

purple bathing suit, climbing out of the water behind me. She had a Southern accent.

"Yeah," I replied, wrapping my towel around me, "it was fun. I didn't even realize how tired I was getting."

"Oh, just you wait till tonight," the girl said, grinning. "Then you'll really feel it. I'll tell you, I sure do."

"Have you been in Girls' Lap Swim for a long time?" I asked, shaking the water out of my ears.

"Well, only 'bout a month," she answered. "But I just love it, don't you?" She lowered her voice. "Tell you a little secret — I didn't even want to join at first. But my daddy insisted on getting me involved in something when we moved here. Said he wanted me to meet other girls." She laughed. "It was either this or tap-dancing lessons."

"Where did you move here from?" I asked.

"Lilletville, Texas," she said, grinning. "Now, don't you tell me you didn't notice my accent. Y'all are always making comments about it up here."

"Well, uh . . ." I began. I didn't want to make her feel self-conscious about the way she talked or anything.

"Come on now, no need to be shy about it!" she bellowed, giving me a little poke in the arm with her elbow.

"I guess I did notice," I admitted, laughing. Suddenly it seemed like nothing could make this girl feel self-conscious about anything. "By the way," I said, "my name is Allison. Allison Cloud."

"Well, howdy, Allison Cloud," she said, beaming. "I'm Tory Wickers."

She pulled off her purple bathing cap, and a huge mane of bright red hair came cascading down her back.

"Wow," I said. "How'd you fit your hair up in that cap? I felt like I was fighting to get all mine in."

"Oh, this is a special oversize bathing cap," she explained. "I ordered it from a catalog. I'll be sure to bring in the catalog for you next time so you can take a look."

"Thanks a lot," I said. "That would be great."

Just then David blew his whistle for our attention, so I sat down next to Tory on one of the tiled benches that surrounded the pool.

"Now we have a very special treat," David told us. "I'd like to introduce Rachel Boland, one of the other instructors here at the Y. Rachel will explain what we're going to see."

A short, young dark-haired woman in a blue warm-up suit stood up.

"Hi, everybody," she said. "As some of you may know, we recently started a Synchronized Swimming Club here at the Y. And I'm here today to try to talk some of you into thinking about joining. Now, I realize that some of you might not be too familiar with synchronized swimming, so I've asked two of the girls in the club, Melanie and Stephanie Peters, to give us a little demonstration."

Melanie and Stephanie stood up and walked over to the pool.

"Oh, don't you just think those two are the cutest?" Tory whispered loudly at my side as the twins lowered themselves into the pool.

"I just met them today," I whispered back. "They seem really nice."

"Synchronized swimming — now, isn't that a little like water ballet or something?" whispered Tory. "I think I saw it in an old movie once or something."

I shrugged. Actually, I wasn't too sure what synchronized swimming was.

Rachel Boland walked over to a shelf mounted on the wall and pressed a button on the stereo system there. As the music began, Stephanie and Melanie struck a pose about waist-deep in the water with their arms outstretched. Then they suddenly dived backward into the water. To the rhythm of the music, they did the backstroke across the pool, stopping at exactly the same moment. Then they dived underwater again and went into a handstand on the bottom of the pool. They opened their legs into splits and closed them again at the exact same time, then went straight into a somersault. It was amazing how they managed to do absolutely everything at the same time, even when they were underwater. A few moments later, when they finished in the same standing position they had started with, the whole room broke out into applause.

"Well, knock me over with a feather!" Tory exclaimed. "Wasn't that the most beautiful thing you ever did see, Allison Cloud?"

"It was amazing," I agreed, nodding. "They were so together — and so graceful."

"Thank you very much, girls," Rachel said as the twins climbed back out of the pool. "Now, I hope you'll all think about joining the Synchronized Swimming Club. We're always looking for new members, and almost anyone who can swim can learn synchro. I know it may look difficult, but all you really need to know is how to float on your back and your stomach, tread water, and to do some basic strokes. The rest all comes with practice."

Tory turned to me.

"Well, what do you say, Allison Cloud?" she asked excitedly.

"What do you mean?" I asked in return.

"Why, the Synchronized Swimming Club!" she said. "Are we in?"

I looked at her. Suddenly I had a vision of myself floating effortlessly through the water, gliding from one graceful movement to the next.

"Definitely!" I said, enthusiastically. I stood up. "Come on, Tory, let's go talk to Rachel Boland about it right away."

# Chapter Six

"So, Allison, tell us all about it," said Sabrina excitedly. She popped a french fry into her mouth.

"Yeah, Al, what's the scoop on the swimming?" asked Randy. She took a sip of her milk shake.

"Did you like the class?" Katie wanted to know.

It was Monday afternoon, and we were all sitting in a booth at Fitzie's after school.

"It was great," I told them. "Really fun. At first I was a little nervous, because I didn't know anybody there and I wasn't even sure if I was a good enough swimmer to be in the class. But then I met some people, and I had a good time."

"What were the other kids like?" asked Sabs, taking a sip of her soda.

"Oh, they were really nice," I answered.

"First I met these really cute twins."

"More twins!" said Randy. "Cool. Maybe they should meet Sabs and Sam."

"Melanie and Stephanie are identical twins," I explained. "You wouldn't believe it — they look exactly alike. It's amazing."

"What about the class?" Katie asked. "Was it hard?"

"It was definitely a lot of work," I said. "I was exhausted when I got home. But I really loved it. And we've got this nice coach. His name is David Steele."

"Sounds terrific, Al," said Randy.

"Oh, and I met this other girl, from Texas," I went on. "She's really funny. Her name is Tory, and she's got this great Texas accent and totally amazing long bright red hair."

"We're just really happy that you found a way to get in shape that you really enjoy, Allison," said Katie.

"It sounds like you had a great time," said Sabs.

"That's for sure," I said. "And that's not all. At the end of the class there was this demonstration of synchronized swimming."

"What kind of swimming?" asked Sabs.

"Synchronized," said Katie. "It means doing something at the same time as someone else. Like when I was on the synchronized skating team for the Winter Carnival."

"That's right," I said. "And you should have seen it. It was really great. Stephanie and Melanie gave the demonstration, and they were really good. In fact, I liked it so much, I decided to join the Synchronized Swimming Club at the Y."

"Wow, Al," said Randy. "Sounds like you're going to be pretty busy."

"That's right," I went on. "The club meets once a week. Rachel — she's the synchro coach — says she wants us all to continue taking Girls' Lap Swim with David twice a week to help us work on our strokes and build up our endurance."

"Synchronized swimming is an official competitive sport, isn't it, Allison?" asked Katie.

"Yes," I said. "At least that's what Rachel told us. But actually, I don't really know all that much about it yet. All I know is that it looks incredibly fun. The first meeting is tomorrow afternoon, though, so I guess I'll learn more about it then."

The next day after school, I hurried to the Y and changed into my bathing suit. When I walked out to the pool, I could see that the lane dividers were gone. Several girls were already sitting on the floor, gathered around Rachel. Tory waved to me and patted the empty space beside her.

"Hi," I whispered as I sat down next to her.

There were eight girls in the group, including the two of us and the Peters twins. I recognized a couple of people from my Lap Swim class.

"Okay, everybody," Rachel said. "We're going to start with some exercises on land first. These should help make the muscles you'll be using in the water stronger and more flexible. It's also important to be stretched out before you get in the pool, to help keep your muscles from cramping up in the water."

She led us through a short warm-up of stretching and strengthening exercises. At first my body was still a little bit sore from all the swimming I had done on Saturday, but the more I stretched, the better I felt.

"All right, now it's time to do some warm-ups in the water," Rachel said. "Everybody in

the pool."

We all got into the water, and Rachel asked us to perform a few short versions of the drills that David had had us do on Saturday — crawl, backstroke, breaststroke.

"Okay," she said. "Now we're going to pair up and start working on some of the specific positions and figures of synchronized swimming. I'll be assigning you a partner with a similar height and build. It's always a little easier to swim together if you have roughly the same-size stroke. And it will also look better to an audience when we decide to have an exhibition."

I felt a little shiver run up my spine. The idea of being in a show made me feel a little nervous, but really excited, too.

Of course, Melanie and Stephanie were paired together, and I wasn't too surprised when Rachel paired me up with Tory. After all, we were both tall, with pretty long arms and legs.

Next, Rachel showed us some of the basic body positions of synchronized swimming. She explained that there were actually twenty-two of them. They were used as the basis for a ton more movements, which were called "figures." Rachel said there were a lot of figures we could learn to do just by mastering a couple of positions first.

The first two positions she had us work on were the back layout and the front layout. These were basically just floating on your back and on your stomach, but you had to keep your toes pointed and completely stretch out your body. When you were on your back, you were supposed to keep your face, thighs, and the tops of your feet right at the surface of the water. It was definitely a lot harder than it looked. Tory and I were both having problems with our legs sinking below the top of the water, so Rachel told us to take turns supporting each other's legs.

"Take a deep breath of air into your lungs, girls," Rachel instructed. "That should help you stay afloat."

After a while both Tory and I managed to do it on our own. The next thing Rachel showed us how to do was called "sculling."

"Sculling is very important in synchronized swimming," she explained, "because it's one of the main ways we move through the water."

She demonstrated the different hand and

arm movements for sculling headfirst through the water, for sculling feetfirst, and for stationary sculling, which helps keep you afloat when you aren't moving at all.

"Jumping jackrabbits!" Tory said with a sigh as we practiced sculling together. "This sure is a lot more complicated than regular old swimming!"

"Now I'm going to have you do an exercise in swimming together in pairs," Rachel announced. "We're going to work on a short routine of swim strokes only. I'd like each pair to practice swimming the length of the pool together using the following sequence of strokes — two front crawls, two sidestrokes, two backstrokes, two sidestrokes, and repeat."

Tory and I held on to the side of the pool and listened.

"The most important thing to do in this exercise is to stay together," Rachel told us. "Do your best to try to swim at the exact same pace as your partner."

I looked at Tory.

"Ready?" I asked.

"Ready as I'll ever be!" she said, grinning. "What did she say — front crawl, sidestroke, backstroke, sidestroke?"

"That's right," I answered. "Two front, two side, two back, two side — two of each."

"Okay, let's go," said Tory.

It was definitely a lot harder than I had expected. Even though Tory and I had the same-length arms, and were at about the same level of swimming, there were some strokes that I did a little faster, and some that she did a little faster. It was hard to stay together. I did notice that Melanie and Stephanie were really good at this, and I realized it must really help when the two partners knew each other so well.

The next thing I knew, Rachel was ending the practice session. Once again, I couldn't believe it was time to stop.

"Very nice work, everyone," Rachel was saying. "Now, remember, the more swimming you do, the stronger you'll be at synchronized swimming. The pool is open early in the morning for any member who wants to work out."

Right away I decided that I was coming back first thing the next morning to swim a few laps before school. It was funny. Even though I was completely exhausted from the workout, I couldn't wait to get back in the pool.

As Tory and I headed toward the locker room together, she turned to me.

"Now, don't you let me forget to give you that catalog before we leave," she said. "You know, for the swim cap."

"Oh, right, thanks," I said. "I could definitely use that."

"Sure thing," she said. She looked at me. "You know, Allison Cloud, that's not all you could use."

"Huh?" I asked. "What are you talking about?"

"I think what you need is a nickname," she told me.

"A nickname?" I repeated. "Why?"

"Well, Allison's just too long a name," she said. "I mean, it's real pretty and all, but it's too formal to go around asking people to say all the time. Why, just about everybody back in Lilletville has a cute little nickname. It kind of saves people from having to use up all their wind power, if you know what I mean. Does everybody always call you Allison?"

"Well," I said, "sometimes my friends at school call me Al."

"Al?!" Tory repeated. "Why, whoever gave

you that nickname? You're definitely too pretty for a name like Al! "

I giggled. It was true, Al did sound sort of big and burly, when you thought about it. And I had certainly never asked anyone to call me Al. It had just sort of happened.

"Why, you as an Al is about as silly as me as a Vic," she said.

"Vic?" I asked.

"Sure," she answered, "my real name's Victoria. But I'm not about to let anyone call me Vic. Tory's much nicer, don't you think?"

I nodded.

"Al!" she said again, shaking her head. "Doesn't anyone ever call you anything else?"

I thought a moment.

"Well, sometimes my mom calls me Allie," I said.

"Allie!" she said, beaming. "That's it! Don't you like that better?"

I thought about it. I had always liked it when my mom called me Allie. And somehow, Allie did sound a lot cuter and more feminine than Al.

"You're right, Tory!" I said, smiling. "From now on I'm Allie."

## Chapter Seven

A week later, at the next meeting of the Synchronized Swimming Club, Rachel made a really exciting announcement. "I'd like us to prepare to give an exhibition," she said. "You've all been working very well in your pairs, and I'd like each pair to think about putting together a routine to perform."

Tory, who was sitting cross-legged next to me, poked me with her elbow.

"Well, leapin' ladybugs, Allie!" she said. "Did you hear that? You and I are going to be in a show!"

I grinned. Sometimes Tory had the funniest way of saying things.

"Now, each pair is going to have to pick a piece of music that they want to work to," Rachel went on. "And then, of course, you'll want to start thinking about costumes — which should all be waterproof, of course. I recommend starting out with some type of swimsuit and adding on. Meanwhile, today I'm going to start showing you some more challenging moves, which you might want to use in your routines."

After we had stretched by the side of the pool and swum a few laps to warm up, Rachel began teaching us some new figures. There was the Water Wheel, where you started by floating on your back in a back layout and then moved your legs along the surface of the water in a sort of "walking" movement. You ended up turning around in a circle while you were floating on top of the water, with your head as the center of the "wheel." We also learned how to do a couple of different types of somersaults, and a really pretty slow movement called Ballet Leg.

But my favorites were the Dolphin movements. You started in a back layout and sort of dived backward underwater with your back arched, going all the way around in a circle until you were back where you had started. Tory really liked that one, too. In fact, after a little while the two of us got so good at it that Rachel suggested we try a special two-person figure called the Dolphin Chain.

"Okay," Rachel instructed us, "now, both of you start in back layouts, except that Allison, you're going to put your feet against Tory's shoulders, with your ankles near her jaw."

We stretched out together, floating on our backs, and I hooked my feet near Tory's head. It was kind of hard to stay afloat attached to each other like that. But by doing some sculling in place, we managed.

"Now," Rachel went on, "what the two of you are trying to do here is to perform one great big Dolphin circle together. Allison, since you're at the head of the chain, you're going to have to start the movement. Since there are two of you, the circle is going to be a lot bigger than it is when you do a Dolphin by yourself, and it'll probably take a little longer to get around. That means you're both going to have to use a lot of extra power, too."

I took a deep breath and let it out. What Rachel was telling us to do definitely didn't sound easy. I wondered how Tory was feeling, but I couldn't see her face.

"Okay, girls," Rachel told us. "Give it a try."

I took in a big gulp of air and held it. Tilting my head back and arching my back, I began diving backward under the water, with Tory's head still between my feet. I used my arms to propel me the way Rachel had shown us, but it was definitely a lot harder to get around now that there were two of us. Suddenly I felt Tory's head slip out from between my feet — we had lost the position. Reluctantly, I swam back up to the surface and let out my breath.

Tory, who was treading water next to me, grinned.

"Well, I reckon that wasn't exactly a success, was it, Allie?" she said.

"Not exactly," I agreed.

"It's a difficult move," said Rachel, who was still squatting by the side of the pool. "Don't be discouraged if it takes a little while." She stood up. "Okay, class, time's up. Don't forget to pick out some music and start thinking about your routine."

"I guess we'd better get together sometime soon and pick out our music," I said to Tory as we climbed out of the pool.

"Sure thing, Allie," she replied, picking up her towel. "Maybe you should come on over to my place on Saturday after Lap Swim. My daddy's got a collection of music as big as the state of Texas."

"That sounds great," I said.

"Saturday it is, then, Allie," said Tory, grinning. "Oooh, I can't wait. Why, we'll have us more fun than two donkeys on a hayride!"

I grinned back at her. I might not have put it exactly the way Tory had, but somehow I knew just what she meant.

\*\*\*

Tory's house turned out to be a really big, modern place in one of the newer areas just outside Acorn Falls. That was why Tory went to a different school.

From the outside Tory's house looked like someone had stuck together a bunch of giant white triangle- and rectangle-shaped boxes. There were big, unusually shaped windows everywhere.

Tory gave me a tour as soon as we got there, and the inside turned out to be really amazing, too. All the floors were covered with plush white wall-to-wall carpeting, and there was a lot of modern chrome-and-black leather furniture.

"This here's the living room," said Tory, leading me through a huge room with an incredibly high ceiling and a circular skylight.

"Wow," I said. "It's beautiful."

"Come on," she said, leading me up a set of black metal spiral stairs to a balcony that overlooked the living room. "The entertainment room's up here. That's where my daddy keeps his music collection."

We walked into a huge room that was filled with more stereo, video, and TV equipment than I had ever seen. Stacked on chrome shelves from the floor to the ceiling were VCRs, tape decks, CD players, and a bunch of other things I couldn't even identify. And mounted on one of the walls was an enormous TV screen.

"Ohmygosh," I said, looking around. "This is incredible."

"Yep," said Tory, flopping down on the oversize black leather couch, "this here's my daddy's little playground. He's in electronics, you know. TVs, stereos, video games, you name it. He owns a big chain of electronics stores down South — Wickers Electronics — but I don't suppose y'all have heard of it up here."

I shook my head.

"Y'all will soon enough, though. Just you wait," she said, grinning. "That's why we moved up here. My daddy's opening a bunch of new stores in this area."

"That's great. I'll be on the lookout for them."

"One thing I told him, though," Tory went on. "I said, 'Daddy, I hope you're not fixin' to use me in any of your advertisements up North.' You see, back in Texas, I was in all the ads for Wickers Electronics."

"Really?" I asked, amazed. "You mean TV advertisements?"

Tory rolled her eyes.

"TV, radio, magazines, catalogs — you name it," she said. "At first I thought it was kind of fun to be known as Miss Wickers Electronics. But then the business just grew and grew, and the ads just started taking up way too much of my time. Came a point when I thought I'd just die if anyone made me smile and say 'Careful pickers shop at Wickers' ever again!"

I laughed.

"I guess that could start to get on your nerves after a while," I said. "But what about your mom? Why didn't you just ask your father to use her in the commercials instead?"

Tory looked down at her hands.

"My mama died when I was a little baby, Allie," she said quietly. "I never got a chance to know her at all."

Suddenly I felt awful. I had never seen Tory look so down.

"Oh, Tory, I'm really sorry," I said. "I-I didn't know."

She looked up at me.

"Well, really now, how could you be expected to know a thing like that?" she said, pressing her lips together. Suddenly she stood up. "My daddy keeps his music over here," she picked up brightly, opening a cabinet in one of the shelves. "How about you and I give a listen to a few things and try to find us something we like for our routine, Allie?"

We spent the next hour listening to different kinds of music. Tory hadn't been kidding about her father's music collection — he had more CDs, tapes, and albums than I had ever seen in one place. We listened to several jazz, rock, country, and classical selections before settling on a really pretty classical piece. It was from an album of Vivaldi music called *The Four Seasons*. As soon as we put it on, both Tory and I agreed that the part called "Spring" was just right for our routine.

"'Spring,' I like that," said Tory. "Y'all have too much cold weather up here anyway. Why, back in Texas, we used to go swimming at Thanksgiving!"

"Really?" I asked, amazed. "Acorn Falls usually gets some snow by Thanksgiving!"

"Snow?! Brrrr." Tory shivered. "I'll tell you, I don't know how y'all can stand the cold. If I were you, I'd just be hankering for spring all winter long."

"Well, it does start to get to you after a while," I admitted. "People in Minnesota are usually pretty happy to see spring once it gets here." I thought a moment. "Hey, Tory, I have an idea!" I said suddenly. "Let's make spring the theme for our synchro routine. After all, it's already the theme of our music."

Tory brightened.

"Let's get ourselves a couple of spring-green bathing suits to wear," she suggested.

"And decorate them with green sequins and stuff," I added.

"And some flowers for our hair," said Tory excitedly. "We can get some of those plastic ones."

"That sounds really pretty. But don't we have

to wear our swim caps?"

"Not if we fasten our hair up real snug. Rachel says as long as it's completely off our faces, it's fine."

"Great!" I said happily. "Oh, Tory, I love this idea."

"Me too, Allie," she agreed, grinning. "And I'll tell you what else. My daddy's having a big grand opening party for his new store at the Widmere Mall a week from Friday. Maybe you and I can go over there a little early with him, do some shopping for our costumes while he's getting his place set up, and then go to the party afterward. It ought to be a real big bash. My daddy likes to do things Texas style — big!"

"That sounds great, Tory," I said. "And listen, there's something else I wanted to talk to you about."

"Sure, Allie. What is it?"

"I really think we should try to put that Dolphin Chain figure into our routine," I told her.

"Jumping jackrabbits, Allie, we can't do that one!" Tory cried.

"I bet we could learn it if we really worked on it, though," I said.

Tory looked at me, and said, "All right there, Allie, you've got yourself a deal. We'll work on that Dolphin Chain like two dogs working on an old chicken bone."

I laughed.

"In that case, I'm sure we'll be able to do it," I said.

Tory looked at me again.

"You know," she said, "I believe you're right. Something tells me you and I were just made to work together, Allie."

# Chapter Eight

A week later Tory and I had worked out our routine. We showed our ideas to Rachel, and she liked them a lot. By the time we had practiced with our music a few times, I was starting to feel really good about it. The only real problem was that Dolphin Chain figure. Both Tory and I were determined to keep it in the routine, but we still hadn't managed to do it. I was definitely getting to be a much stronger swimmer, though. In fact, David Steele had moved me out of the slow lane by my third Lap Swim class.

The date of the exhibition was creeping up on us, and I was so busy with swimming that I hardly had time to do anything else. Practically the only time I had to see Sabs, Katie, and Randy was in school.

On Friday at lunch, Sabrina sat down at our table in the cafeteria.

"Wow," she said, "another one of your

grandmother's feasts."

"I bet you could feed the whole cafeteria with what you've got in that bag," cracked Randy.

"Actually, lately I haven't felt like these lunches are so big after all," I said, hungrily taking a bite of my turkey-and-oat-bread sandwich. "These days, I feel like I'm always hungry."

"That's probably because of all the exercise you're doing," said Katie. "You're using up more energy, so your body needs more food as fuel."

"I know," I said. "At least that's what Rachel says."

"Rachel?" asked Randy.

"Rachel's our coach, remember?" I answered.

"I thought Dave was your coach," said Sabrina.

"David coaches Girls' Lap Swim, and Rachel coaches the Synchronized Swimming Club. Anyway, Rachel says that we should try to make carbohydrates sixty to sixty-five percent of our diet. You know, like pasta, cereal, potatoes, rice, and bread."

"Isn't that stuff fattening?" asked Sabs.

"Not really," I explained. "Rachel says that

those are the highest-energy foods. And they give you the highest fiber for the lowest amount of calories. And, of course, you have to eat some protein and other stuff, too. But what you're really supposed to be careful about is avoiding fat. That means even though potatoes are in, greasy french fries are out."

"No more Fitzie's fries?" asked Randy, amazed.

"Not until after the exhibition, at least," I answered.

"Wow," said Sabs, "it seems like you're really devoted to this whole thing, Al."

"Oh, by the way, that reminds me," I said. "I've been thinking, and I'm not so sure I really want to be called Al anymore."

"Why not?" said Randy. "You've always been Al."

"Well, not really," I said. "I mean, no one ever calls me that at home, for example."

"I guess that's true," said Katie.

"So you mean you want us to just try to call you Allison all the time?" asked Sabrina.

"Well, actually," I began, "Tory and I were talking, and we came up with an idea."

"Tory from Texas," said Randy.

"Right," I said. "Anyway, Tory asked me why I had picked Al as a nickname, and I started to realize that I hadn't ever really chosen it — it was just something I ended up getting called sometimes."

"But we thought you liked Al, Al," said Sabs.

"Well, I never really gave it much thought before," I answered. "But Tory and I were talking, and I mentioned to her that at home my mom sometimes calls me Allie."

"You mean you want us to start calling you Allie?" asked Katie.

"It's just that I kind of think it sounds a little more feminine," I explained.

Katie, Randy, and Sabs looked at each other.

"I guess it is a little more glamorous than Al," said Sabs. "You know, it's kind of like an actress's name — like Ally Sheedy or Ali MacGraw."

"I don't know if I can get used to this, Al," said Randy. "I mean, Allison, or Allie, or whatever."

"It might be kind of hard to suddenly start calling you something different," said Katie.

"Well, all I'm asking you to do is try," I said,

a little exasperated.

"You're right, Allison," said Katie. "You should be able to be called whatever you want."

"Really," agreed Sabs. "If that's what you want, we'll try to remember."

"Well, it shouldn't be any more difficult than getting volunteers for the next recycling drive," joked Randy. "Nothing's tougher than that."

"Oh, that's right!" I said suddenly. "The SAFE meeting next week — I almost forgot!"

SAFE is the name of the environmental club I formed at Bradley. It stands for Student Action for the Environment. Once a month, we hold a big recycling drive in school. So, a few days before the drive, I always call a SAFE meeting to try to get people to volunteer to help sort the bottles, cans, and newspapers.

"The meeting's next Thursday, right?" asked Sabrina.

I thought a moment.

"Um, I think so — I mean, definitely," I said. "I've been meeting Tory at the pool every day after school to practice our routine, but I'll just tell her I'm going to be a little late that day."

Randy, Katie, and Sabs looked at each other, and I felt kind of strange all of a sudden. But the bell rang, and soon I didn't have time to wonder what they were thinking.

The week flew by. Between the regular Girls' Lap Swim sessions, the Synchro Club meetings, and extra rehearsals with Tory, I was incredibly busy.

After Lap Swim on Wednesday, I ran into Marnie Hooper in the lobby of the YWCA, and she told me she had just signed up for an exercise class. It made me really happy to know that Marnie was getting herself in shape, too. Who knew, I thought, maybe by the time we had to take the National Fitness Exam next year, Marnie and I might be among the top scorers.

On Thursday, the members of SAFE gathered after school in the empty classroom where we hold our meetings. As I sat down on top of the desk in the front of the room, Arizonna, this really cool guy in our class from California, smacked his forehead with his hand with a look of surprise.

"Allison Cloud!" he exclaimed. "Haven't seen much of you around lately. How goes it?"

"Hi, Arizonna," I said, smiling. "I guess I've been a little busy."

"So what's up?" asked Sabrina's brother

Sam. "What's this meeting all about, anyway?"

"Sam!" said Sabs, exasperated. "Don't you remember anything? It's almost the first Monday of the month — we have to organize the recycling drive!"

"Ugh!" groaned Sam.

I looked at my watch — three-twenty. I had told Tory I would be at the pool by four o'clock.

"Okay," I began, "I'm in a little bit of a rush, y'all, so let's see if we can get this done quickly."

Suddenly, I noticed Randy, Sabs, and Katie looking at me with kind of funny expressions on their faces.

"If we can just get us four volunteers for the recycling drive," I went on, "why, I'll be as happy as . . . as . . . a donkey on a hayride."

Suddenly everyone stared at me.

"A donkey on a hayride?" repeated Sam.

"Whatever," I said. "The point is, we need four volunteers for the recycling drive" — I looked at my watch — "and we need them pretty quick. Now who's ready to volunteer?"

After a little bit of pushing on my part, four kids finally volunteered.

"Okay, y'all, thanks a lot," I said, writing

their names down in the green notebook that I use to keep SAFE's records.

I glanced at my watch. Three-forty. If I hurried, I would still make it to the Y by four. I stuffed my notebook into my bag and quickly pulled on my coat. Just as I was picking up my bag, Randy, Katie, and Sabs walked up to me.

"Hey, Allison," said Randy. "I want to ask you something before you go."

"Okay," I said, "but it has to be kind of quick. I'm running a little late."

"No big deal," Randy went on. "It's just that Sabs and Katie and I were thinking. We haven't seen too much of you lately because of this swim thing — "

"Look, I'm sorry, but it's just that I've really had to do a lot of training," I broke in, "especially with this exhibition coming up so soon."

"No, no, that's fine," said Sabrina. "I mean, we understand about the rehearsals and stuff."

"Really," Katie put in. "We know you have to train a lot so you can stay in shape for the exhibition."

"It's just that we'd kind of like to have a chance to see you, too," said Randy. "Which is why I'm going to have a sleepover at my house tomorrow night. Sabs and Katie are coming, and I thought we could all watch videos and get a bunch of ice cream and fudge and stuff and make sundaes."

"I'm sorry, Randy," I replied. "I mean, it sounds like a lot of fun, but I don't think I can make it."

"Don't tell me you have to swim on a Friday night?" said Katie with a sigh.

"No, no, that's not it," I said. "I'm supposed to go to a party with Tory. Her father's having some big grand opening thing at one of his electronics stores."

"Oh, well, then why don't you just tell her you can't make it?" asked Randy.

"I can't," I answered. "I already said I would go. Besides, I want to go — it sounds like it's going to be fun."

"Well, Randy's will be fun, too," pointed out Sabs.

"We can understand that you have to practice a lot, Allison," said Katie, "but do you really have to spend your free time with this Tory person, too?"

"No, I don't," I said, "but I happen to like Tory a lot."

"And what about us?" asked Randy. "Aren't we supposed to be your best friends?"

"You are all my best friends. You know that." I took a deep breath. "Look, I'm sorry I can't make it to the sleepover, but y'all are just going to have to understand."

"You know, Allison, you don't even sound like yourself anymore," said Sabrina suddenly.

"Look," I replied, sighing and looking at my watch, "I don't even know what you're talking about. But I do know that I'm going to be late if I stay here and talk about it anymore."

Before anyone could say anything else, I threw my bag over my shoulder and hurried out the door.

# Chapter Nine

The next day — Friday — after school, I sat in the backseat of Tory's father's huge white car as he gave the two of us a ride to Widmere. Tory sat up front, fiddling with the car stereo and popping different CDs into the CD player built into the dashboard.

"Everything all right back there, little lady?" Mr. Wickers bellowed to me over his shoulder.

"Just fine, thanks, Mr. Wickers," I answered.

Tory's father wasn't like any of the other fathers I had met in Acorn Falls. For one thing, he was incredibly tall. And for another, he wore huge bright red pointy boots with his plain gray business suit. I could definitely see where Tory had picked up some of her mannerisms, too, like poking people with her elbow and saying things like "jumping jackrabbits." Tory was a lot like her father. She even looked like him, except for her hair. Mr. Wickers's hair was jet black. I guessed Tory must have gotten her bright red hair from her mother.

Mr. Wickers let us out in front of the mall entrance before going to park the car.

"Y'all have fun, now, and I'll see you around six o'clock at the store," he said, grinning.

"Let's go look for our bathing suits first, Tory," I suggested as we walked into the mall.

"Okay by me," she answered. "Where should we go? I'll bet you know this place pretty well."

"Oh, sure," I said. "I come here with my friends Randy, Katie, and Sabrina all the — " Suddenly I stopped. Thinking about Randy, Katie, and Sabs made me remember the conversation I had had with them after the SAFE meeting the day before. I started to feel pretty bad about the whole thing.

"Allie, are you okay?" asked Tory, looking at me.

"Yeah, sure," I said, shrugging. "I'm fine."

"Well, you sure don't look fine to me," she countered. "As a matter of fact, you look about as fine as a dog that just met up with a porcupine."

I managed a laugh.

"It's nothing, really, Tory," I said. "It's just a little misunderstanding I had with my friends at school yesterday."

"Looks like they must be pretty good friends, if you ask me," she said. "I mean, for you to be that down in the dumps about it."

"They are," I told her. "As a matter of fact, they're my very best friends in the whole world. But after yesterday, I'm not so sure they still know it."

"What happened?" asked Tory. "Did y'all have a fight or something?"

"Not really," I answered. "At least, I don't think so. It's just that I've been so busy with synchro lately that I haven't had too much time for them." I paused. "And I think they also might be kind of upset because I'm spending time with you," I added.

"Well, leaping ladybugs, Allie," said Tory, "those friends of yours just aren't used to sharing you is all. You give them some time, and they'll come around. Why, I think they're lucky as bees in a flower shop to have you as a friend."

I smiled. There was definitely something about the way Tory said things that cheered me up.

"Come on," I said, leading her toward the escalator. "Let's go upstairs to the Sport Shop and see if they have any spring-green bathing suits."

Twenty minutes later, we had picked out two matching bright green tank suits and were on our way to JoAnn's Hobby Shop to look for things to sew onto them.

"Maybe after this we can stop and get a snack somewhere," I suggested. "I'm starved."

"Jumping jackrabbits, Allie, you don't want to eat anything now!" she said. "Why, I told you, my daddy likes to do things Texas style — that means big! There's going to be more food at that grand opening party than there are ants at a picnic!"

"All right, all right," I said, laughing. "I guess I can wait a little while longer. Come on. Here's the hobby shop."

We went inside and began looking through the huge selection of ribbons, sequins, beads, and other decorations. Finally we picked out some pretty green sequins to sew onto our bathing suits.

"These should look real nice and sparkly in the water," said Tory.

"Look over here," I said, waving her over to a basket full of plastic flowers. "Let's pick some out for our hair."

"Oooh, Allie, this color looks beautiful with your black hair," she said, eagerly pulling an orange tiger lily out of the basket and holding it up to my hair. "What kind should I wear, do you think?"

"I like these," I said, holding up a deep blue iris.

We each bought three flowers for our hair. Then, as we were walking out of the store, Tory suddenly stopped in her tracks.

"What is it?" I asked. "What's wrong, Tory?"

"Listen," she said, looking up into the air.

"What?" I said, listening. Suddenly I realized what she was talking about.

"Our song!" we both cried.

It was true — they were playing a version of Vivaldi's "Spring," the song we were using for our synchro routine, over the sound system at the mall. Before we knew it, we were both moving our arms in time to the music, imitating the motions we made during our routine. It was a little difficult with no water, but somehow we managed to do something like our whole routine together, staying in synch the whole time. I had to admit, it felt pretty funny to be dancing around in the mall like that, and a few people were definitely staring at us, but mostly it was just a lot of fun.

"Mark my words, Allie," Tory cried, giving me a little hug as we finished, "this here is a sign. I just know you and I are going to do real well on Sunday at that exhibition!"

"I think so, too, Tory," I said, hugging her back.

"Come on," she said. "We better head on over to my daddy's store. The festivities ought to be just about in full swing by now."

We walked through the mall until we came to Wickers Electronics, which had taken over the big empty store that had once been Sanderson's Furniture. There was a huge banner across the front window that said GRAND OPENING, with red, white, and blue streamers hanging all over the place. Two clowns with bright orange wigs stood outside the store, handing out red, white, and blue fliers to people who passed by, and I could hear loud music coming from inside.

"Let's go on in," said Tory, leading me past the clowns and into the store.

Inside, country music was blaring from what seemed like a zillion huge speakers attached to the ceiling, and there were people everywhere. Some stood around eating food off red, white, and blue paper plates, while others were actually shopping and looking at the merchandise. A juggler in a court-jester suit walked by me, tossing red rubber balls into the air. And across the room I could see an organ grinder, complete with a real monkey.

"Wow!" I yelled to Tory above the music. "This is unbelievable!"

"Come on!" she yelled back. "Let's go find my daddy and say hey."

I followed her as she wove her way through the crowds of people. We passed two more jugglers and a belly dancer before we finally found Mr. Wickers, in a huge white apron over his business suit, serving hot dogs and hamburgers at a huge table covered with a red-and-white-checkered tablecloth.

"Hey there, Daddy!" Tory called as we made our way over to him.

"Hey there, Tory!" he called back, beaming. He looked at me. "Hey there, little lady, get yourself a plate and start digging into some of this here food — put a little meat on those bones of yours."

I laughed, suddenly thinking of my grand-mother.

"Don't mind my daddy," said Tory, as we grabbed two plates. "He's always saying stuff like that."

As we loaded up on hot dogs, hamburgers, potato salad, coleslaw, and corn on the cob, she turned to me.

"Oh, Allie, I plumb forgot to tell you the good news!" she said suddenly.

"Good news?" I repeated.

"Only about as good as a flyswatter in a swamp!" she said, laughing. "My daddy's fix-ing to give the Synchronized Swimming Club a little present — a set of underwater speakers."

"Oh, Tory, that's great!" I said excitedly. "That means we'll all be able to hear the music for our routines under the water."

"That's right, Allie. He's having it installed for us tomorrow. That way we'll be able to use it for the show on Sunday."

"Wow," I said, "it's really lucky for the Synchro Club that your father decided to open a store up here."

"Well, you know what they say," said Tory, a twinkle in her eye.

"Careful pickers shop at Wickers!" we sang out together, laughing.

## Chapter Ten

"Well, Allie," Tory said grinning at me, "I guess this is it."

"Here," I said, "let me pin those flowers in your hair."

It was Sunday afternoon, the day of the exhibition, and the girls of the Synchronized Swim Club were all in the locker room of the Y, getting ready. Tory and I were dressed in our matching green bathing suits with the green sequins, and we had pulled our hair into tight buns on top of our heads.

I knew my family was waiting out by the pool, sitting in the bleachers that had been set up for the show. I hadn't spoken to Randy, Katie, and Sabs since Friday, but I had invited them to the exhibition. I hoped they were coming.

Just then, Rachel came into the locker room and gathered us all around her.

"Okay, girls," she said, "here we go. Now, as you may know, Tory Wickers's father has been kind enough to donate a set of underwater speakers to us. They've been installed, and I've tested them, and they're working just great. They should really make things a lot easier for you."

I smiled at Tory, and she grinned back at me.

"Before we start," Rachel went on, "I just want to tell all of you that I'm really proud of you. You've worked very hard these past few weeks, and I think we've really put together a terrific show. So, good luck, everyone!"

"Good luck, Allie," said Tory, giving me a hug.

"Good luck, Tory," I said, hugging her back.

After we had all wished each other good luck, I got a double hug from Melanie and Stephanie Peters. Then we filed out of the locker room and down the blue-tiled hallway toward the pool.

I tried not to look at the bleachers, which were filled with people, as I took my seat next to Tory on one of the tiled benches with the other swimmers. Suddenly, I had a nervous feeling in my stomach. Tory must have felt the same way, because just then, she reached out and grabbed my hand and gave it a little squeeze. I squeezed back, and took a deep breath, which made me feel a little better.

Rachel stood up and faced the bleachers.

"I'd like to welcome you all to the first exhibition of the Acorn Falls Synchronized Swim Club," she said. "The girls you see behind me have worked very hard on what they are going to present to you today, and we should be very proud of them all. So, please relax and enjoy the show!"

The first routine to be presented was Melanie and Stephanie's. As they stood up and walked over to the pool in their matching yellow bathing suits, I could hear the crowd in the bleachers begin to murmur, and I knew everyone must be talking about how alike they looked.

As usual, Melanie and Stephanie performed their routine beautifully, and it seemed like they were completely together at every move. But what I was really impressed by was how calm they looked. Somehow, even in front of all those people, they managed to keep identical, relaxed smiles on their faces. When they finished, they got a lot of applause from the audience.

The next two girls, wearing red sparkly bathing suits, performed a pretty fast routine to a rock song. They did pretty well, too, although at one point one of them sped up a little and ended up finishing her somersault ahead of the other.

Then Tory poked me with her elbow.

"Come on, Allie," she whispered loudly, "we're up."

I stood up and walked toward the pool, taking deep breaths to calm my stomach. Suddenly, I was worrying about all kinds of things. What if I forgot the routine? What if Tory and I didn't stay together, in synch? And most of all, what about the Dolphin Chain? What if we couldn't manage to do it?

As I climbed down into the pool, I happened to glance up at the bleachers. There, sitting in the third row with my parents, my grandparents, and my little brother, were Katie, Sabrina, and Randy! I caught Randy's eye, and she winked and flashed me the "thumbs-up" sign. Suddenly, I felt much better about everything. As Tory and I took our starting places in the pool, it was a lot easier to smile than I had thought it would be.

The first part of our routine went really smoothly. It was definitely a lot better being able to hear the music both above and below the water, and Tory and I were able to stay together perfectly.

Then it was time for the Dolphin Chain. Tory and I went into our back layouts, and I hooked my feet around her head. We sculled in place for a couple of moments, and then I gave her the signal we had worked out — wiggling my toes against her shoulders. I took a great big breath and held it, feeling Tory's shoulders rise as she did the same.

Tilting my head back, I dove backward under the water with my back arched. I could feel Tory's head between my feet as I propelled myself back and under with my arms as hard as I could. The next thing I knew, I had completed the circle, and my face was at the surface of the water. A moment later, Tory surfaced, and the two of us were back in our original back layout position, with my feet still against her shoulders. We had done it — a perfect Dolphin Chain!

I couldn't stop smiling as we did the rest of

our routine. When we were finished, there was a burst of really loud applause.

"Jumping jackrabbits, Allie," Tory whispered loudly as we got out of the pool, "we did it!"

Her voice must have really carried in that huge room, because suddenly the audience began to laugh. Tory turned to me and shrugged, but I couldn't help noticing that there were two bright-pink spots on her cheeks. It seemed like something could actually make Tory Wickers feel a little embarrassed after all.

As we took our places on the bench with the other swimmers, I felt really happy. So happy that I barely even noticed the last pair of swimmers doing their routine.

As soon as it was over, though, we were suddenly surrounded by people. Everyone poured out of the bleachers and surrounded all the swimmers, congratulating them. I saw my parents making their way toward me through the crowd.

"Oh, Allie," my mother said, giving me a quick hug. "That was marvelous!"

"Very impressive work, Allison," added my father.

Charlie ran up to us, dragging my grandparents behind him.

"You were great!" he sang out happily.

"Fantastic, little girl!" said my grandfather.

"We're all proud of you," added my grandmother.

"By the way," said my mother, "Mary Birdsong said to tell you that she wished she could have been here, but she's home with Barrett, who was fussing a little. Mary wanted me to give you these, though."

She held out a beautiful bouquet of yellow roses.

"Wow," I said, taking them from her, "these are really pretty."

Suddenly I felt something soft and warm draped over my shoulders. I turned around and saw Katie, Sabrina, and Randy standing behind me.

"Oh, thanks so much, you guys," I said, wrapping the plush pink towel more tightly around me and smiling at them. "A towel — great. I was starting to get kind of cold."

"Hey, this isn't just any towel, though," said Randy, grinning.

"Really," said Sabrina.

"Look closely," said Katie, smiling.

I looked down at the towel and noticed that there was something purple near one of the edges.

"What's this?" I said, turning it so I could read it.

There, along the edge of the towel, embroidered in really pretty purple script was the name "Allie."

Suddenly, I felt like I was about to cry.

"You guys are the greatest," I said, looking at them.

"No, Allie, you're the greatest," said Randy. "We just wanted to let you know that we're really sorry about everything that happened after the SAFE meeting the other day."

"Really," added Katie. "We realized it was wrong of us to get so upset."

"After all," said Sabrina, "you should be allowed to have other friends, too."

"Actually," said Randy. "I'd kind of like to meet that girl Tory sometime. She seems kind of wild."

"Really," said Sabrina, giggling. "What was that thing she said — jumping jackrabbits?"

I looked over at Tory, who was standing with

her father and a few other people. She glanced back at me and gave a little wave.

"Well, come on, and I'll introduce you right now!" I said happily.

Suddenly I felt like the luckiest person in the world. I had made a really neat new friend, and I had discovered an incredibly fun hobby. But best of all, I knew for sure that I had the three best friends anyone could ever ask for.

## Don't Miss
## Girl Talk #35
## KATIE AND SABRINA'S BIG
## COMPETITION

"What's that?" Sabs asked, stopping next to me.

"It's a poster for a triathlon event," I answered, still scanning the print. "It's going to be held at the new Acorn Falls Sports Complex three weeks from tomorrow. It sounds really cool!"

I began to read the interesting parts off to Sabs. "It's for kids ages seven to fourteen. They'll be broken down into two groups, Juniors, who are seven-to-ten-year-olds, and Seniors, who are eleven-to-fourteen-year-olds. There's going to be a girl winner and a boy winner for both groups, and the prize for first place is a one-year membership to the sports complex!

"There's a 200-meter swim, a 6-mile bike ride, and a 1.2-mile run," I went on. I could feel myself getting really excited as I looked at my friends. "Doesn't that sound great? I can do all those things. I'm going to sign up!"

"I'll sign up, too!" Sabs chimed in. "That way we can do it together. It'll be really fun!"

*Fun* wasn't exactly a word that came to mind when I thought about training. It was definitely challenging, and satisfying, though. Maybe that was what Sabs meant.

"It's going to take a lot of hard work and training," I told her. "I mean, the triathlon is the hardest event you can participate in!" I didn't want to scare her or anything, but I wanted to make sure she knew what she was getting into.

"So you don't want to do it anymore?" Sabs asked, looking disappointed.

"I still want to do it," I said quickly.

"Well, then I want to do it, too," she said emphatically. "We can train together! It'll be fun, Katie, you'll see. Now let's go over and check out those new neon workout clothes."

I followed quietly as she pulled me toward the workout clothes. Sabs was probably right. It would be fun training for the triathlon with a partner.

So then why was there a niggling doubt in the back of my mind?

# TALK BACK!
## TELL US WHAT YOU THINK ABOUT
## GIRL TALK BOOKS

Name _____

Address _____

City _____ State _____ Zip_____

Birthday _____ Mo._____ Year _____

Telephone Number  (____)_____

**1)** Did you like this GIRL TALK book?

Check one:  YES_____  NO_____

**2)** Would you buy another GIRL TALK book?

Check one:  YES_____  NO_____

*If you like GIRL TALK books, please answer questions 3-5;*
*otherwise go directly to question 6.*

**3)** What do you like most about GIRL TALK books?

Check one:  Characters_____ Situations_____
           Telephone Talk_____Other_____

**4)** Who is your favorite GIRL TALK character?

Check one:  Sabrina_____  Katie_____  Randy_____
Allison_____  Stacy_____  Other (give name) _____

**5)** Who is your *least* favorite character?

_____

**6)** Where did you buy this GIRL TALK book?

Check one: Bookstore____Toy store____Discount store____
Grocery store___Supermarket___Other (give name)_____
*Please turn over to continue survey.*

**7)** How many GIRL TALK books have you read?
Check one:   0_____   1 to 2_____   3 to 4 _____   5 or more_____

**8)** In what type of store would you look for GIRL TALK books?
Bookstore_____Toy store_____Discount store_____
Grocery store_____Supermarket_____Other (give name)_____

**9)** Which type of store would you visit most often if you wanted to buy a GIRL TALK book?
Check *only* one:    Bookstore_____Toy store_____
Discount store_____Grocery store_____Supermarket_____
Other (give name)_____

**10)** How many books do you read in a month?
Check one:   0_____   1 to 2_____   3 to 4 _____   5 or more_____

**11)** Do you read any of these books?
Check those you have read:
The Baby-sitters Club_____  Nancy Drew_____
Pen Pals_____ Sweet Valley High _____
Sweet Valley Twins_____Gymnasts_____

**12)** Where do you shop most often to buy these books?
Check one:    Bookstore_____Toy store_____
Discount store_____Grocery store_____Supermarket_____
Other (give name)_____

**13)** What other kinds of books do you read most often?
_____

**14)** What would you like to read more about in GIRL TALK?
_____
_____

Send completed form to :
GIRL TALK Survey, Western Publishing Company, Inc.
1220 Mound Avenue, Mail Station #85
Racine, Wisconsin 53404

**LOOK FOR THE AWESOME GIRL TALK BOOKS IN
A STORE NEAR YOU!**

# MORE GIRL TALK TITLES TO LOOK FOR

*Nonfiction*
**ASK ALLIE** 101 answers to your questions about boys, friends, family, and school!

**YOUR PERSONALITY QUIZ** Fun, easy quizzes to help you discover the real you!

**BOYTALK: HOW TO TALK TO YOUR FAVORITE GUY**